# For the love of Chatoyer

## Elliot King

AuthorHouse™ UK
1663 Liberty Drive
Bloomington, IN 47403  USA
www.authorhouse.co.uk
Phone: 0800 047 8203 (Domestic TFN)
+44 1908 723714 (International)

Because of the dynamic nature of the Internet, any web addresses or links contained in this book may have changed
since publication and may no longer be valid. The views expressed in this work are solely those of the author and do
not necessarily reflect the views of the publisher, and the publisher hereby disclaims any responsibility for them.

Any people depicted in stock imagery provided by Getty Images are models,
and such images are being used for illustrative purposes only.
Certain stock imagery © Getty Images.

This book is printed on acid-free paper.

ISBN: 978-1-7283-9820-4 (sc)
978-1-7283-9819-8 (e)

Print information available on the last page.

Published by AuthorHouse  01/31/2020

authorHOUSE®

# Foreword

Good attempt captures the imagination of the young fresh approach.

Curtis King
Headmaster St. Vincent Grammar School West Indies

# Ode to Chatoyer

Chatoyer! Chatoyer!,
The sun is rising

Chatoyer! Chatoyer!,
Our warriors are waiting

Chatoyer! Chatoyer!,
Our love for you is enduring

Chatoyer! Chatoyer!,
Great chief your bravery is outstanding

Chatoyer! Chatoyer!,
Your restored our pride

Chatoyer! Chatoyer!,
To you the honour, we humbly step aside

Chatoyer! Chatoyer!,
Our hopes, our fears in you abide

Chatoyer! Chatoyer!,
This island Hairoun, our home

Chatoyer! Chatoyer!,
From the mountains to the sea, our ancestors did roam

Chatoyer! Chatoyer!,
With free spirits, we love this land the sea and forest loam

# For the love of Chatoyer

Chatoyer stood on the brow of the hill flickering a fly from his arm, gazed at the distant horizon below him, the blue Caribbean sea, flowed along the coastline of St. Vincent, in the distance he could see the island of St. Lucia covered by mist. The second half of the 17th century was in the progress. Not yet a man, hoped to follow his father and continue the outstanding line of warriors, that his family had produced, related to him by his grandfather. He imagined himself as a great warrior, leading the Caribs into battle to protect his country in which he loved. Choosing a wife, especially Maka the daughter of the Carib chief Dupant, whom he had fallen in love with, and was on his way to visit her in a secret hiding place near the village where they met before. She had given him a lock of hair, and in return gave her an English brooch, which he found many years ago. Keeping mainly to the mountain areas Chatoyer continued his Journey, avoiding the coastal areas as much as possible where many of the sugar plantations were located belonging to the white English men who brought with them black men and women that harvest the cane. These people spoke a language called English and belonged to a religion called Christianity, they had succeeded in converting a small number of Caribs, and built churches to worship, arriving on the island in very large ships. His father who had learnt some English at the Garrison, passed what he had learnt down to him, so that he was able to understand some very basic words, but was determined to continue learning in order to express himself in the future, because recently there was anger between the English settlers and the Caribs regarding the allocation of Carib lands without the permission of the Caribs, resulting in, the Caribs burning several cane plantations. The midday sun beat down on the lush tropical landscape. To the east, the dense forest covered the hilly terrain sloping towards the valley leading down to the sea. On the black sandy beach several canoes lay in neat rows, adjacent to the sea. Chatoyer walked quickly, stopping briefly to hunt the wild agouti that fed on the forest floor and was lucky to kill one. He knew that Maka was fond of the meat, and would be pleased with his offerings. He hoped that she had remembered to meet him, in their secret hiding place, located between and jagged rocks, leading to a secluded cave. He had not seen Maka since the last moon, and hopedshe had kept her promise to be there. Arriving at their intended destination, Chatoyer scanned the area, looked around the bushy undergrowth, but Maka was nowhere to be seen perhaps he thought, she had forgotten her promise and decided not to come, because of some other reason. As he stood pondering, he felt soft hands, clasp his eyes, and knew it was Maka, turning around their eyes met, followed by rapturous laughter. They sat on the side of the protruding rock. "Look what I have for you Maka!" Chatoyer stated indicating, the agouti lying in the bush. "Someday you will be a great warrior and hunter, and I would give you many sons and daughters, my love, for you is like the moon lighting up the darkness, for you and me, two hearts beating as one, across the length and breadth of our beloved homeland", Maka replied. Chatoyer smiled, the compliment was gratifying even more sincere was her revelation of love for him which made him a very happy person, whatever the future held for him, he would need courage, determination and humility. His time with Maka now and in the future will be very essential and important. The time had come to say goodbye to Maka, it had been a pleasant and enjoyable time for them. The time passed swiftly, later, towards evening Chatoyer and Maka walked towards Maka's village separating at the fork.

Chatoyer started on his journey home, looking back briefly, waved to Maka, she acknowledged his gesture waved back throwing flower petals in the air, disappearing behind the large stone mound. Chatoyer walked quickly, he realized that he had to get home quickly. Darkness was fast approaching although he walked as fast as he could, realized that all his effort was futile after taking a wrong path, ended up on a cane plantation, decided to spend the night in a cluster of trees, hoping that the English owners would not pass his way during the night. Chatoyer set out on his journey home at daybreak, after spending an uncomfortable night halfway up a cedar tree. Tired and hungry he finally arrived at his village, greeted his family, ate a large meal, retired, at his hammock and fell asleep. A sudden commotion woke Chatoyer, rising to his feet walked towards the centre of the village. A large group of Caribs stood exchanging views verbally, he could tell by their tone of voice that they were angry. Enquring of his brother the reason for the gathering was told that the Caribs chiefs and warriors, had come together to vent their feelings of anger at the English settlers and others, being given Carib lands without the permission of the chiefs. In return the Caribs had decided to start an insurrection across the island. Chatoyer joined the crowd as the meeting progressed. The chiefs agreed that every village must select their best fighting men and attack the settlers as a united force. The meeting over, Chatoyer followed his father to their hut.

As Chatoyer grew to manhood, his father taught him the essentials of warfare, demonstrating the use of weapons, including the musket, given to his father by his cousin in St. Lucia. He realized the importance of preparing himself for the future. He was well developed, agile, and the best hunter in the village. In a few weeks he would be a man, and hoped to be selected for the insurrection, it would be a great honour to serve his country and people, which he dearly loved, and would give his life protecting it. Two days later his father told him that he was selected with others from his village. Chatoyer was jubilant at last he was on his way to achieving his dreams knowing that there would be danger and life threating situations but he was willing to take the risk. The Carib chiefs stood in the middle of the large group of warriors. The group was further divided into sections. Each selection had a commander in chief responsible for attacking the settler's in different area of the island, retreating back inot the forest causing as much damage as possible. Chatoyer listened and watched as the chiefs used small stones to illustrate their plan of action. The meeting concluded, the warriors dispersed. Chatoyer joined the warriors of his section, on daily skirmishes with the settlers, gaining experience, developing as a very tactful warrior, as he partook in launching attacks, on the sugar cane plantations, and as a result was held in high esteem by warriors and elected Carib chief.

The day had come for the Caribs liaison with the French who had captured the island from the British. Dressed in their ceremonial attire, they proceeded to Kingstown to meet with the French administration. Chatoyer was hoping, that the meeting would give the Caribs a much needed Ali who could engage the English on equal terms, the chiefs had decided to allocate some Carib lands to the French, as a gesture of good will. The Caribs were delighted, the French were good hosts, providing a sumptuous lunch followed by French wine which the chiefs had never tasted before Madae Celeste, the wife of a plantation owner in Martinique was fascinated by, Chatoyer and suggested that he pose for a painting which she would commission with a French artist in Martinique. Overwhelmed by the constant attention payed to them by the French, the Caribs finished their meal and departed in the late afternoon to their various locations.

Maka was waiting for Chatoyer as he arrived back at the village. Heavily pregnant, approached, showering him with yellow petals. Chatoyer smiled, it had been a good day, and he had seen for himself how the white people lived. Entering the hut, he sat down. Maka had prepared a feast, his family had gathered with others in anticipation of receiving details of his visit. "Was the French ladies like English when I was younger, I saw an English lady, walking in Kingstown I hid among the bushes so she could not see me, what was the inside the English house like, I am very curious," Maka said bringing a murmur from those present, "Well it is not like our hut, the rooms were large decorated with ornaments paintings of which one of them was their king in France, chairs to sit on around a large polished table, where we had our food and drinks especially the strong French wine it makes you feel strange when you drink too much, you become talkative, and merry, I had to restrain Baptiste, he almost fell over, as he got up from the table, I had to hold him so as not to embarrass us". Everyone laughed, Chatoyer then continued explaining the remaining details of the visit and concluded that the Frenchmen will be the Caribs allies in the future. The feast finished, the participants departed, Chatoyer and Maka made their way into the interior of the hut. "I would like to visit my family especially my father and mother, it's been a moon on two, since I last saw them, I know like you are a chief with many responsibilities, I would like you to come with me and spend time at our secret meeting place, I know they could be pleased that I am with child." Maka remarked. "I will go with you and hunt some agoutis, on the way there." Chatoyer replied smiling broadly.

A week later at dawn. Chatoyer and Maka began their journey to the windward side of the island, walking between the lush flora and fauna that covered both sides of the winding path, along the mountainous terrain arriving at Maka's village in the afternoon. They were greeted with chants as Maka's family and others surrounded the couple in jovial adoration. A feast followed lasting into the moonlit night. Chatoyer awoke late, Maka was asleep, bleary eyed stood up and walked towards the entrance to his hut, as the golden rays of early morning sun encroached the village, in the hut nearby he could see some of his family members already awake perhaps going on a hunt. Chatoyer and Maka splashed in the cool clear river water as they frolicked, a message was delivered inviting Chatoyer to his cousins wedding in St. Lucia. He was delighted, it would be his second visit to St. Lucia his first, was before he become a man. Now, that he was a chief the benefits would be good, as the Frenchmen who ruled in St. Lucia may be able to help him with future military campaigns against the English, especially the use of muskets and other areas of warfare, Captain James G. Morgan unbuttoned the top of his uniform. The heat was unbearable. He had been used to the cold damp climate in England especially witner, where he lived with his wife and two sons. He had joined the army at an early age, served his country well in military campaigns, promoted to sergeant then captain due to his exceptional performance and tactical skills in warfare. He was then sent to the island of St. Vincent in the West Indies to take command of the colonial militia in view of protecting the settlers and interest of England, particularly the sugar plantations that was in danger of an insurrection by the indigenous Carib people. However as time passed by he got used to island life especially the mosquitoes which plagued him daily so far, he had been able to pacify some of the Carib leaders but recently the Caribs began attacking and killing settlers across the island. The colonial militia was outnumbered by the Caribs, his job was to confront the Caribs on the windward side of the island in view of protecting the settlers especially the sugar cane plantations a very valuable asset to England as sugar was in great demand as many merchants and plantations owners grew rich on the proceed of the sugar industry. He knew his life could be ended at any time during the campaign and decided then to write a letter to his wife in England.

The rain began to fall a little at first then a torrential downpour. Looking through the window observed the buildings of the colonial militia, in a cluster adjacent to a dirt road providing access to the town centre. Darkness began to descend over the landscape, bowing his head continued writing the letter.

Chatoyer, carefully arranged his ceremonial attire, and entered a large canoe decorated and containing specially selected gifts for his cousin in St. Lucia, and waved to his warriors as the boat glided slowly over the oncoming waves and faded from sight. Chatoyer yawned he could see the coast of St. Lucia, soon the skilled oars men navigated the narrow passage between the inlet, bringing the canoe to a halt beyond the reef. Chatoyer disembarked followed by the oarsmen, made his way to the almond tree where his cousin and others were waiting. A joyous reunion took place resulting in him being carried to his cousins' village. The wedding feast began towards the afternoon Chatoyer was introduced to other Carib chiefs in St. Lucia, including two French officers who also attended the feast and welcomed him as a friend insisting that he visit their headquarters the following day. Chatoyer was pleased, he thanked the Frenchmen for their kindness and agreed to meet them, knowing that they could teach him and his warriors, the use of weapons including the muscket. The feast progressed into the early hours of the morning. Chatoyer and his cousin where the last to leave, walking slowly between the dying embers of the fires towards the huts at the end of the village. Unable to sleep, Chatoyer woke early as they grey canopy of dawn began to usher in tinges of blue in the sky, his thoughts led to Maka who was pregnant with their third child. It had been a wise decision to come St. Lucia, he was due to meet the French officers at midday. He knew how crucial the meeting would be as he needed the help of the French in the near future in view of training his warriors and perhaps joining the Caribs in the war with the English who had superior weapons and armory. The Caribs knew the terrain, the dense forest and could use guerrilla attacks on the English with some success as he found out with his recent skirmish with the English. He had seen his beloved Hairoun change when more settlers arrived slowly alienating the Caribs and annexing the land. The meeting between Chatoyer and the French army representatives was a cordial and successful event, the French reiterate their support for the Caribs in St. Vincent. Two days later Chatoyer arrived back at home pleased with his visit to St. Lucia.

Chatoyer sat under a tree surrounded by his family, pipe in hand, he related stories told by his grandfather, to a time when Caribs roamed free on the island. It was a time when there were no cane plantation very few English people. As he spoke to a messenger arrived stating that Caribs chief Duvalier and others wished to get together to form a battle plan for war against the English, having reached a conclusion to engage the English in battle throughout the island. Chatoyer was pleased with the outcome of the meeting. The time had come for his people to declare that they would not be harassed, or made inferior in their own land, they would fight to the end, and he knew it was now or never, the English were growing stronger, more settlers were arriving on the island. The forts were being reinforced, the Caribs had to strike first using the cover of the forest to launch periodic attacks, coordinating them between the Carib chiefs on the island. He also realized that it would not be an easy task, as the English had superior weapons and would get reinforcements from England. Chatoyer smiled, it was a happy day for everyone. Maka had given him another son, another warrior to fight against any people that wished to dominate the Caribs in the future. A future that must assert the Caribs as master of their own land, not as subjects of another race. He felt that if they lost the war, the Caribs way of life would be lost forever unless of course they were victorious with the help of the French. This was the only way forward for the Caribs. The preparation for the war had gone very well. The warriors were eager and had followed the instructions of the French officers. Carib chief Duvalier had made arrangements for surprise attacks on English fortifications across the island in two days' time. The attacks were to be coordinated simultaneously on the windward and the leeward side of the island.

The long voyage from England was over for Major Alevander Leith. He had spent, most of the time in his cabin, it was the first time and he had been on such a long sea voyage to the island of St. Vincent in the West Indies to the colonial militia, which was stretched to the limit, requiring reinforcements from England. The warlike indigenous Caribs were killing settlers and burning sugar cane plantations which was a valuable commodity to the British government and others involved as sugar fetched a high price in England and owners of the plantations and merchants grew rich on the proceeds. Standing on the deck major Leith looked towards the shore, the emerald green vegetation hilly terrain in the distance. A long boat arrived and pulled up beside the ship as the waiting soldiers in a neat line, disembarked. He was the last to leave stepping cautiously into the already crowded boat. The oarsmen rowed the boat towards the shore and the waiting crowd on the jetty. It was the end of his journey from England, but the beginning of a new chapter in his life. As they stepped ashore the governor his aides, and soldiers from the colonial militia welcomed them.

Maka woke suddenly, she had a terrible dream, in which Chatoyer and her were walking along the valley floor, suddenly a storm arose, and they ran and sheltered in a cave, but Chatoryer dropped his pipe and went back to retrieve it, suddenly a bolt of lightning struck him. She ran to help him, but he was already dead. Panicking she realized he was not in his hut, rushed outside, her heart pounding she saw him smoking his pipe under his favourite tree. She approached him touched his hands, body and face her voice raised in joy "Chatoyer" Chatoyer my love, my love "you are here". "yes I am here Maka, you are acting strangely is something wrong?" "I had a bad dream and I was afraid when I opened my eyes and you were not lying beside me, I panicked but now I am happy." The Carib warriors assembled at day break in Chatoyer's village in anticipation of the imminent attack on the English this time it would be war. The pent up anger they felt towards the English settlers were growing day by day and was ready to follow their chief into battle, regardless of the outcome. Chatoyer knew that as the other leader he had the full support of his warriors who idolized him, but the majority of them were familiar with the terrain loyal and brave. The time for negotiations with the English had passed, they had welcome the strangers from across the seas in brotherhood and friendship allowing them to settle and plant their sugar canes. As the time passed, they began to usurp the Caribs authority, which brought anger and conflict especially with the English. Chatoyer addressed the warriors, a loud cheer followed, as they brandished their weapons into the air, families watched and cheered.

Captain Morgain yawned, flicking a fly from the lapels of his uniform, rehearsing in his mind what he was going to say to his soldiers, standing in neat lines in bright sunshine on the parade ground. The Caribs had begun burning, killing, and plundering settlers on the sugar cane plantations. The settlers had requested assistance from the governor, as they were fearful and vulnerable. Reinforcements were requested from England to join the "colonial militia", and was due to arrive on the island in a few weeks' time. Walking briskly towards the soldiers addressed them pointing out the dangers they could face, engaging the Caribs in battle, as they were good fighters, mounting his horse, he led soldiers through the streets of Kingstown on their way to "Three Rivers" situated in the windward side of the island. The hot sun, accompanied by the incessant contact of insects made progress difficult, colliding on the bodies of the soldiers as they made their way in the forested areas, finally stopping at the nearest cane plantation before continuing their journey. It was necessary for his men and himself to spend the night, as the Caribs could use the darkness for surprise attacks. Early the next morning captain Morgan and his men, resumed their journey being very cautious at the Caribs were masters of disguise, they knew the terrain could be waiting to ambush them however, it was a risk that they had to take, many of his men were raw recruits never travelled to foreign lands especially to tropical destination with the heat and humidity and a different way of life to what they were used to, in England. Passing through the thick undergrowth along the narrow trail, the horses became restless, as they emerged into a larged clearing at the bottom of a hill, a volley of musket fire rained down on the unsuspecting soldiers causing panic, as the Caribs shot and wounded soldiers and disappeared into the forest. Captain Morgan, then decided the best course of action was to take his wounded and dead soldiers back to Kingtown in view of treating and burying them.

Chatoyer exhausted lay down on the coarse matting floor, it had been a long but a successful day, a day which resulted in victory over the English in many areas, especially on the windward side of the island where the Caribs were able to stem the advance of English causing casualties. The French had been a good ally joining the Caribs in battle against the English. So far the war had gone very well, his warriors had fought valiantly some had died, but the remainder had proved that they were a force to be reckoned with. His thoughts drifted to maka and his sons, who had gone to stay with her mother and her family in their village as they would be safer there. As commander in chief he was able to access and concentrate on the areas where the English were vulnerable, using guerrilla warfare when necessary, which had been very successful. More English soldiers had arrived on the island, and assumed that more will follow. Knowing that it would become impossible unless they completely defeated the English and were masters again on their beloved "Hairoun" to achieve this, he was willing to lay down his life, to fight to the end, for love of his people and his homeland, was as deep as the ocean and high as the stars in the sky. He was proud of his eldest son, who like him was a good warrior and orator being able to speak and write English and French and was a valuable asset in communicating with the English And Frenchmen. He missed Maka, but knew she was safe with her family and well hidden in the deep forest, knowing that she would be thinking about, however as commander in chief of the Caribs his time would be spent mostly in battle, that will ultimately decide the destiny of his people. In the distance an owl hooted and he fell asleep.

Major Alexander Leith woke early breaking over the silent landscape, kneeling on the carpeted floor, of the chapel opened his bible, and prayed, rising to his feet, wrote a letter to his wife in England. Although the English army had the advantage and had pushed the Caribs back in key areas with the reinforcements of the way. The Caribs had proved to be resilient and were victorious in many areas, especially on the windward side of the island. Chatoyer had led them in a unique guerilla attack aided by the French soldiers whose support could make the war harder to win especially if reinforcements were sent to help the French soldiers and the Caribs. He longed to return to England, but knew that in war, death was always present to any soldier, in any army. He did not dislike the islands of the Caribbean, especially St Vincent, he was treated kindly with great respect by the colonists and felt appreciated more than in England. He admired the beauty of the island, the tropical land and seascape, and drew sketches in his notebook to take back to England.

Chatoyer musket in hand, led his Carib soldiers through the thick undergrowth on the leeward side of the island to link up with Duvalles' men, who were positioned at Marriaqua valley and Fairbairn's ridge. He attacked an English contingent sent for relieving of the Vigie who retreated with many dead, fled in the direction of Prospect and Villa leaving the Vigie in Caribs hands. Chatoyer was cautious his plan was to get closer to Kingstown the capital, knowing that the English soldiers will soon recapture the Vigie, His strategy was to surround Kingstown knowing it would be a difficult task as the English were getting stronger. Selecting a group of warriors, whom he felt was excellent in the guerrilla warfare, Chatoyer decided to go to Kingstown and execute attacks on the English soldiers in view of weakening their defenses, Chatoyer and his warrior walked quickly, avoiding the settlements and main trails that led to Kingstown. Dusk was fact approaching as they took up a position to the west of Kingstown where they hoped to launch their attack.

Major Alexander Leith mounted his horse and led his soldiers to the west of Kingstown he needed to reinforce the section as it was forested and could give the Caribs the advantage in attacks. As his soldiers climbed a steep ridge, a band of Caribs attacked them, killing some soldiers before they could seek cover. As the both parties engaged in close combat, Chatoyer sprang on Major Leith holding his neck in a brace, reached for his knife, however, Major Leith stuck his elbow in Chatoyer's stomach, the knife and plunged into Major Leith chest

Printed in the United States
By Bookmasters